Where Does the Sun Go at Night?

Where Does the Sun Go at Night?

Adapted from an Armenian song

by **Mirra Ginsburg**
pictures by **Jose Aruego**
and **Ariane Dewey**

Greenwillow Books, New York

The four-color preseparated art was prepared as a black line drawing with halftone overlays for red, yellow, blue and black.

Library of Congress Cataloging in Publication Data
Ginsburg, Mirra.   Where does the sun go at night?
Summary: Every night the sun goes to the house of his
grandma, the deep blue sky, is tucked in bed by his
grandpa, the wind, and is awakened the following day
by the morning.   [1. Sun—Fiction]   I. Aruego, Jose.
II. Dewey, Ariane.   III. Title. PZ7.G43896Wf   [E]   79-16151
ISBN 0-688-80245-1   ISBN 0-688-84245-3 lib. bdg.

To Libby

Where does the sun go at night?

To his grandma's house.

Where does he sleep?

In his grandma's bed.

Who is his grandma?

The deep blue sky.

What is he covered with?

A woolly cloud.

Who tucks him in?

His grandpa.

Who is his grandpa?

The wind.

What does he dream about?

The moon and the stars.

Who wakes him up?

The morning.

Who wakes the morning?

The alarm clock.

Who is the clock?

The village cock.